SUPERMAN FAMILY ADVENTURES

VOLUME 1

ART BALTAZAR
writer & artist
FRANCO
writer

Superman created by Jerry Siegel and Joe Shuster. Superboy created by Jerry Siegel.
Supergirl based on characters created by Jerry Siegel and Joe Shuster. By special arrangement with the Jerry Siegel family.

KRISTY QUINN EDITOR–ORIGINAL SERIES **ROBIN WILDMAN** EDITOR **ROBBIN BROSTERMAN** DESIGN DIRECTOR–BOOKS **DAMIAN RYLAND** PUBLICATION DESIGN

BOB HARRAS SENIOR VP – EDITOR-IN-CHIEF, DC COMICS

DIANE NELSON PRESIDENT **DAN DIDIO** AND **JIM LEE** CO-PUBLISHERS **GEOFF JOHNS** CHIEF CREATIVE OFFICER **JOHN ROOD** EXECUTIVE VP–SALES, MARKETING AND BUSINESS DEVELOPMENT **AMY GENKINS** SENIOR VP–BUSINESS AND LEGAL AFFAIRS **NAIRI GARDINER** SENIOR VP–FINANCE **JEFF BOISON** VP–PUBLISHING PLANNING **MARK CHIARELLO** VP–ART DIRECTION AND DESIGN **JOHN CUNNINGHAM** VP–MARKETING **TERRI CUNNINGHAM** VP–TALENT RELATIONS AND SERVICES **ALISON GILL** SENIOR VP–MANUFACTURING AND OPERATIONS **HANK KANALZ** SENIOR VP–VERTIGO & INTEGRATED PUBLISHING **JAY KOGAN** VP–BUSINESS AND LEGAL AFFAIRS, PUBLISHING **JACK MAHAN** VP–BUSINESS AFFAIRS, TALENT **NICK NAPOLITANO** VP–MANUFACTURING ADMINISTRATION **SUE POHJA** VP–BOOK SALES **COURTNEY SIMMONS** SENIOR VP–PUBLICITY **BOB WAYNE** SENIOR VP–SALES

SUPERMAN FAMILY ADVENTURES VOLUME 1

DC Comics, 1700 Broadway, New York, NY 10019. A Warner Bros. Entertainment Company. Printed by RR Donnelley, Salem, VA, USA. 5/24/13. First Printing. ISBN: 978-1-4012-4050-9

Library of Congress Cataloging-in-Publication Data

Baltazar, Art.
Superman Family Adventures. Volume 1 / Art Baltazar, Franco Aureliani.
pages cm. — (Superman Family Adventures)
"Originally published in single magazine form in Superman Family Adventures 1-6."
ISBN 978-1-4012-4050-9
1. Graphic novels. I. Aureliani, Franco. II. Title.
PN6728.S9B35 2013
741.5'973—dc23

2013009138

SUSTAINABLE FORESTRY INITIATIVE
Certified Chain of Custody
At Least 20% Certified Forest Content
www.sfiprogram.org
SFI-01042
APPLIES TO TEXT STOCK ONLY

DAILY
PLANET

MEANWHILE... IN THE FAR REACHES OF SPACE...
A FIERY METEORITE IS ON A COLLISION COURSE TOWARDS EARTH!
MORE IMPORTANT... METROPOLIS!
BUT WAIT!
WHAT'S THIS?!
LOOK!
UP IN THE SKY!
IT'S A BIRD!
IT'S A PLANE!

IT'S SUPERMAN!
WOW! IS THAT A NEW SUIT?
I REALLY LIKE THE NEW V-NECK COLLAR!
I CAN'T BELIEVE HE CAUGHT THAT!
COOL! HAVEN'T SEEN HIM IN A LONG TIME!
SUPERMAN FAMILY ADVENTURES
TIME TO SEND THIS ROCK...
...BACK INTO SPACE!
NOW, TO ADD A LITTLE BIT OF HEAT VISION...
EXPLODE!
ZAP!
...AND DISINTEGRATE THE ROCK INTO HARMLESS PEBBLES!

WHILE BACK AT THE DAILY PLANET...
DAILY PLANET
KENT!
KENT! WHERE'S KENT?!
PERRY WHITE
HERE I AM! WHAT DID I MISS?
PERRY WHITE
SUPERMAN, KENT!
You MISSED SUPERMAN AGAIN!
NO WORRIES, CHIEF. I GOT THE SCOOP!
LOIS LANE! THAT'S WHY YOU'RE MY BEST REPORTER!
You COULD LEARN A LOT FROM HER, KENT!
RIGHT, CHIEF.
PERRY WHITE
Y'KNOW CLARK, YOU'RE NEVER HERE WHEN THERE'S ACTION ABOUT!
MAYBE IT'S BECAUSE I'M REALLY SUPERMAN, LOIS.

OH, CLARK KENT. YOU'RE SUCH A JOKER!
MAYBE GOTHAM CITY IS MORE YOUR STYLE.
BOOM!
ROBOTS?!
WHAT IS IT WITH METROPOLIS?!
SOMETHING'S ALWAYS HAPPENING HERE!
OLSEN!
YES, CHIEF?
GET ME THOSE PHOTOS!
RIGHT, CHIEF!
LANE!
GET ME THAT STORY!
RIGHT, CHIEF!
OLSEN!
WHERE'S MY COFFEE?
OLSEN!

YOU JUST SENT OLSEN OUT TO TAKE PHOTOS, SIR.
OH, RIGHT.
WELL, TEXT HIM TO BRING MY COFFEE ON HIS WAY BACK!
KENT!
KENT!
CLARK KENT?!!
WHERE'D HE GO?!
HE'S NEVER AROUND WHEN YOU NEED HIM!
ROBOTS STOMPING METROPOLIS?!
THIS LOOKS LIKE A JOB FOR...
DAILY PLANET
SUPERMAN!

OKAY, YOU ROBOTS!
WHAT ARE YOU DOING HERE IN METROPOLIS?
WHAT DO YOU WANT?
WHY ARE YOU SMASHING THINGS?
E
X
L
MAIL
THROW!
MAIL
I MEAN... THROWING THINGS?
TALK ABOUT EXPRESS MAIL!
CATCH!
MAIL
MAIL
THROW!
CATCH!
MAIL
I SEE YOU'RE INTO FAST CARS, TOO!

WE'RE HERE, COUSIN KAL!
WE HEARD THE BIG BOOM WITH OUR SUPER HEARING!
GREAT, KIDS!
BE CAUTIOUS! THESE ROBOTS ARE DANGEROUS!
SMACK!
CRASH!
WHOA!
AND SMART, TOO!
FIRST, YOU THROW THINGS AT ME?
THEN, SLAP ME AROUND?
NOT COOL.
SO, YA WANNA PLAY?

HOW ABOUT A GAME OF...
...THROW THE ROBOT INTO SPACE?!
HELP!
OH, NO! JIMMY'S IN TROUBLE!
HELP!
STOMP!
CLICK CLICK
STOMP!

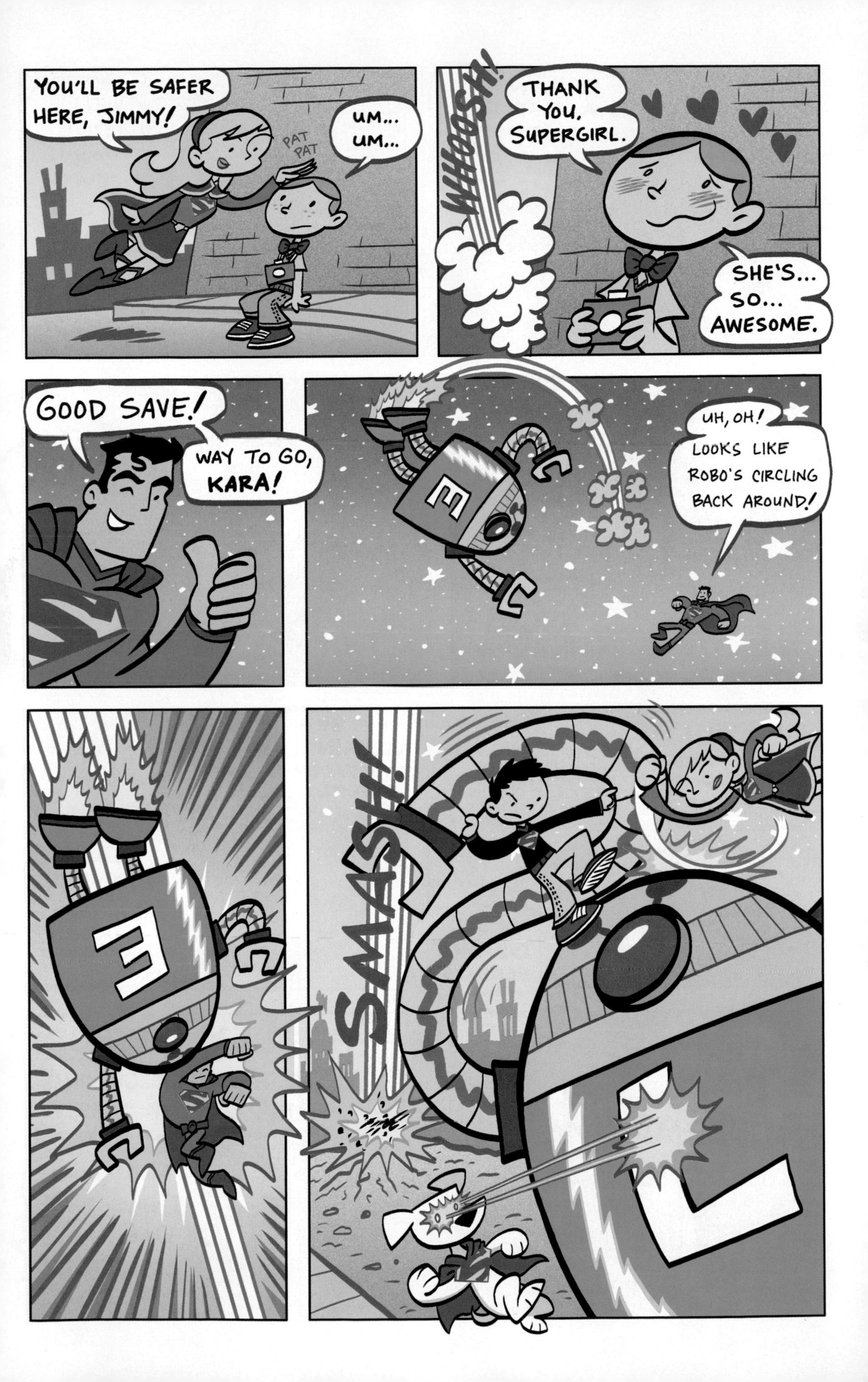
YOU'LL BE SAFER HERE, JIMMY!
PAT PAT
UM... UM...
WHOOSH!
THANK YOU, SUPERGIRL.
SHE'S... SO... AWESOME.
GOOD SAVE!
WAY TO GO, KARA!
UH, OH! LOOKS LIKE ROBO'S CIRCLING BACK AROUND!
SMASH!!

UGH. WHAT A HARD FALL!
OUCH!
WELL... ONE DOWN, TWO TO GO!
HEY!
GRAB!
SQUEEZE!
THE EVIL EYE? IT'S LIKE SOMEONE IS LOOKING BACK AT ME!
BUT, WHO?
AN EVIL GENIUS PERHAPS?
MUST BE A VILLAIN I'VE FACED BEFORE!
DEFINITELY SOMEONE WITH VAST KNOWLEDGE OF ROBOTIC TECHNOLOGY!
THAT'S RIGHT, SUPERMAN!
IT'S LEX LUTHOR, THE GREATEST CRIMINAL MIND OF OUR TIME!
AND SOON I WILL HAVE ALL YOUR POWERS!
!!!!

SQUEEK!
FUZZY? WHAT ARE YOU DOING OUT OF YOUR CAGE?
I UNDERSTAND YOUR NEED TO BE CLOSE TO LEX LUTHOR'S KEEN INTELLECT!
LEX LUTHOR'S SAVVY!
BUT YOU MUST REMAIN IN YOUR CAGE!
NOW, WHERE WAS I?
THAT'S RIGHT! SUPERMAN'S POWERS!
A MERE FLIP OF THIS SWITCH WILL ACTIVATE THE ABSORPTION RAY I'VE INSTALLED IN MY ROBOT'S HEAD!
THEN, I WILL DRAIN THOSE KRYPTONIAN POWERS AND TRANSFER THEM TO...
MY LUTHOR BATTLE SUIT!
HA! HA! HA!
KIND OF GIVES YOU A CERTAIN SHUDDER OF ELECTRICITY JUST BEING IN THE SAME ROOM WITH ME, HUH?
SQUEEK!
EXACTLY!

MEANWHILE, IN METROPOLIS...
ZAP!
CRUMBLE!
FAP!
FAP!
CLICK!
HUH? IT'S A TEXT FROM THE CHIEF.
TEXT
COFFEE?
NOW?
YES, I KNOW HOW YOU LIKE YOUR COFFEE!
TWO SUGARS!
I GET IT!
YOW!
STOMP!
COFFEE
RUN RUN
UM... T...T...TWO S...SUGARS C...C...C... COFFEE!
WHAT HAPPENED TO YOU?
SMASH!!
AAHH!
IT'S ON THE HOUSE!

WHILE AT LUTHOR'S LAIR...
NOW!
THE MOMENT HAS ARRIVED!
HISTORY IS ABOUT TO BE MADE!
FUZZY? OUT OF YOUR CAGE AGAIN?
SQUEEK!
VERY WELL!
YOU ARE ABOUT TO WITNESS THE END OF SUPERMAN AND THE RISE OF SUPER LUTHOR!
SWITCH
ACTIVATE!
BBSSZZZ
VVVMMMMMM
WHA?
SUPERMAN! WATCH OUT FOR THE LASER!

ZAP!
BLOCK!
SUDDENLY, THE ROBOT'S ABSORPTION RAY ABSORBS A PORTION OF KRYPTO'S SUPER POWERS...
...THEN TRANSPORTS THEM THROUGH THE AIRWAVES...
...AND DOWNLOADS THEM INTO LEX'S COMPUTER...
...THEN INTO LEX'S EVIL MACHINE...
...AND INTO THE LUTHOR BATTLE SUIT!
HA HA HA!
IT'S WORKING! I FEEL SUPER POWERFUL ALREADY!
HA HA HA!

I HAVE SUPER STRENGTH!
SUPER VISION!
SUPER FLIGHT!
ALONG WITH MY SUPER INTELLECT, I WILL BE UNSTOPPABLE!
AHEM!
FUZZY?
WHY ARE YOU FLYING?
I THINK I GOT SOME OF THOSE POWERS, TOO!
TALKING? YOU'RE TALKING NOW, TOO?
EXCUSE ME A MOMENT.
SCRATCH SCRATCH
UM...
ENOUGH ALREADY!
AGAIN?
GRAB!
SNAP!

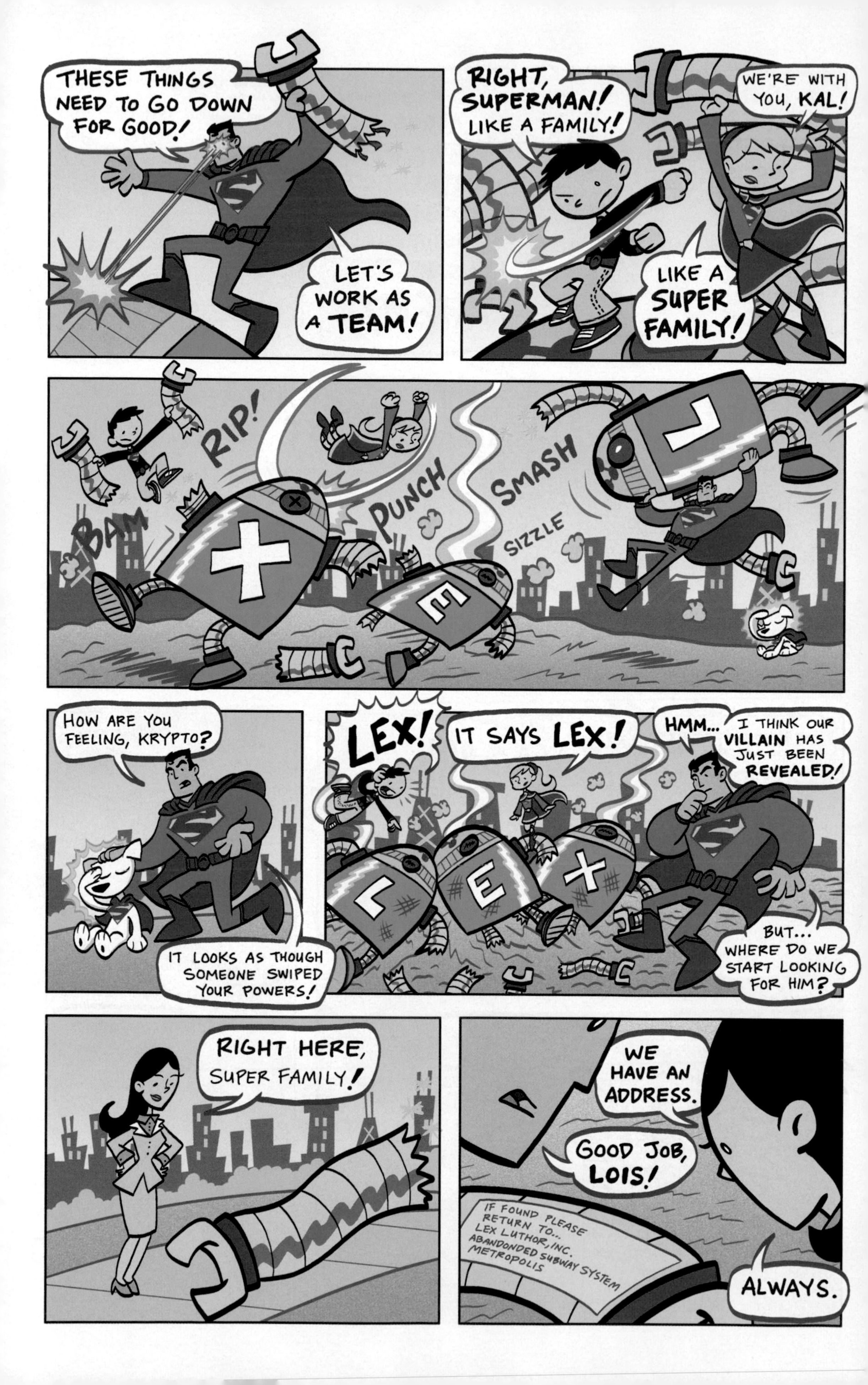
THESE THINGS NEED TO GO DOWN FOR GOOD!
LET'S WORK AS A TEAM!
RIGHT, SUPERMAN! LIKE A FAMILY!
WE'RE WITH YOU, KAL!
LIKE A SUPER FAMILY!
RIP!
BAM
PUNCH
SMASH
SIZZLE
HOW ARE YOU FEELING, KRYPTO?
IT LOOKS AS THOUGH SOMEONE SWIPED YOUR POWERS!
LEX!
IT SAYS LEX!
HMM...
I THINK OUR VILLAIN HAS JUST BEEN REVEALED!
BUT... WHERE DO WE START LOOKING FOR HIM?
RIGHT HERE, SUPER FAMILY!
WE HAVE AN ADDRESS.
GOOD JOB, LOIS!
IF FOUND PLEASE RETURN TO... LEX LUTHOR, INC. ABANDONED SUBWAY SYSTEM METROPOLIS
ALWAYS.

NO NEED TO GO LOOKING FOR ME, SUPERMAN!
LUTHOR!
LEX
I, LEX LUTHOR WILL DESTROY...
BARK! BARK! BARK!
HUH?
UM... KAL? IS LEX BARKING?
YEAH.
LIKE KRYPTO!
BARK?
HEY!
YOUR SUIT MAY BE SUPER, LUTHOR...
RIP!
...BUT YOU ARE NOT!

HERE YOU GO, SUPER FAMILY!
THE MOUSE TALKS?
HIS NAME IS FUZZY!
THANK YOU, FUZZY!
YOU CAN'T DEFEAT ME SO EASILY... YOU!
ARE YOU SURE ABOUT THAT, LEX?
HERE, BOY!
RUFF
BARK
RUFF
GO FETCH!
LOOK WHAT WE FOUND IN YOUR LAIR, LUTHOR!
WHAT?
LEAP
COURTESY OF SUPER SPEED DELIVERY!
LIFT!
ACTIVATE!
BBZZZZZZZ
OPEN

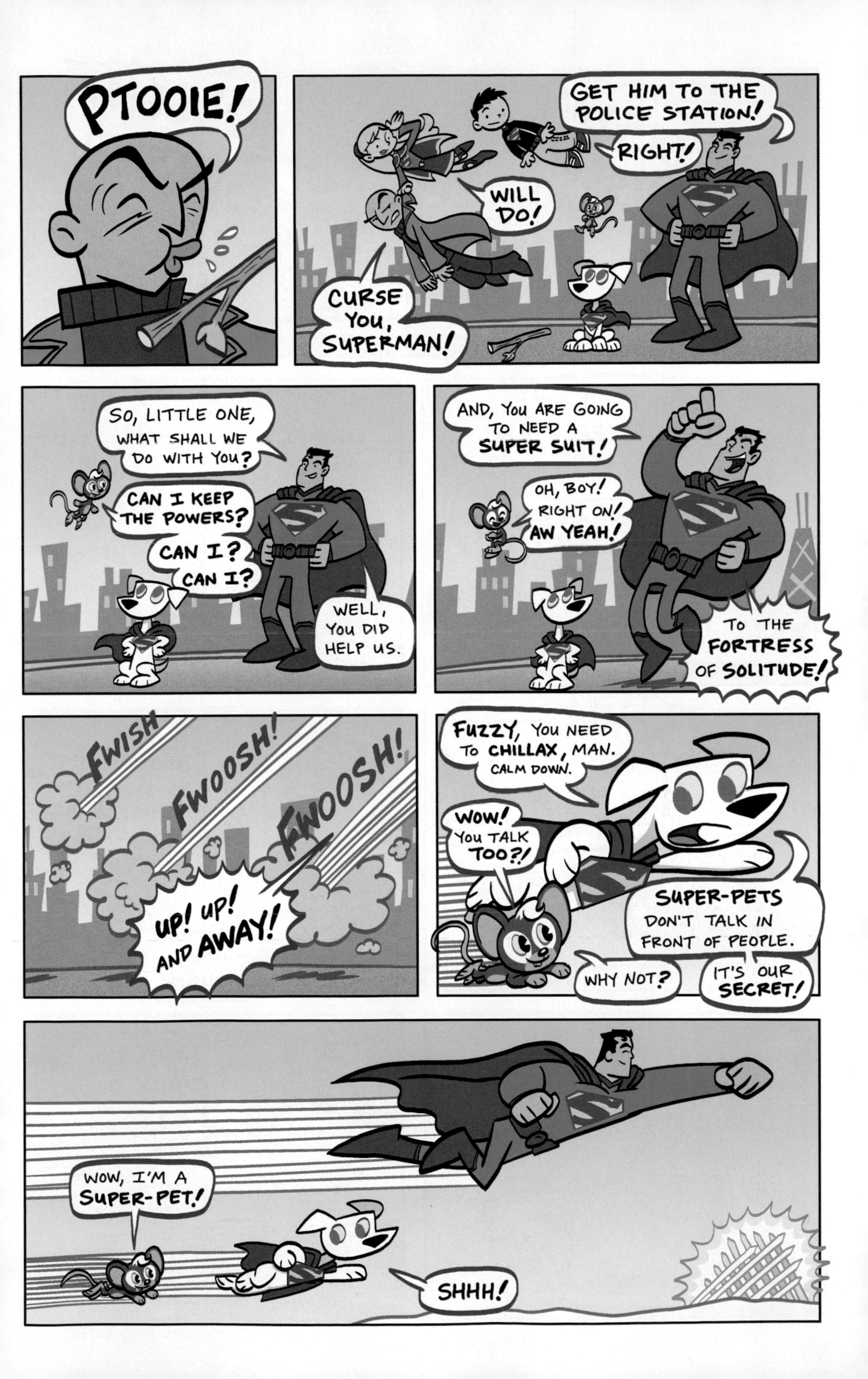
PTOOIE!
GET HIM TO THE POLICE STATION!
RIGHT!
WILL DO!
CURSE YOU, SUPERMAN!
SO, LITTLE ONE, WHAT SHALL WE DO WITH YOU?
CAN I KEEP THE POWERS?
CAN I? CAN I?
WELL, YOU DID HELP US.
AND, YOU ARE GOING TO NEED A SUPER SUIT!
OH, BOY! RIGHT ON! AW YEAH!
TO THE FORTRESS OF SOLITUDE!
FWISH
FWOOSH!
FWOOSH!
UP! UP! AND AWAY!
FUZZY, YOU NEED TO CHILLAX, MAN. CALM DOWN.
WOW! YOU TALK TOO?!
SUPER-PETS DON'T TALK IN FRONT OF PEOPLE.
WHY NOT?
IT'S OUR SECRET!
WOW, I'M A SUPER-PET!
SHHH!

MEANWHILE...
DAILY PLANET
OLSEN! OLSEN!
OLSEN! OLSEN!
PERRY WHITE
HERE, CHIEF.
IS THAT MY COFFEE?
YES, SIR.
WHY AM I NOT HOLDING IT?
PERRY WHITE
DRINK DRINK CHUG
PERRY WHITE
ACK!
IT'S COLD! AND I SAID TWO SUGARS!
OH, THERE'S TWO SUGARS. THERE IS ALSO A LITTLE DUST, RUBBLE, AND ROBOT DEBRIS.
FAIR ENOUGH!
DRINK SIP DRINK
PERRY WHITE
OKAY. CARRY ON.
-DIGGIN' SOME COFFEE, TOO!

PLUS!
FUZZY
THE KRYPTO MOUSE!
GREAT KRYPTON!
WHO IS HE? AND WHY IS HE DRESSED LIKE US?!
ME AM HERE TO JOIN FAMILY!
?!
ENTER:
BIZARRO!
ART BALTAZAR 2012

MEANWHILE, IN THE FAR REACHES OF SPACE...
A SQUARE METEOR ROCK IS ON A COLLISION COURSE WITH EARTH!
MORE IMPORTANT, METROPOLIS!
MEANWHILE IN METROPOLIS...
...WE JOIN JIMMY OLSEN WITH HIS FRIENDS, CHLOE, SONJA, AND FOZ ALREADY IN PROGRESS...
SO GLAD TO HANG OUT WITH YOU GUYS TODAY!
RIGHT! IT'S NOT EVERY DAY YOU GET A DAY OFF!
TEXT
WHA?
MORE COFFEE? NOW?
ON MY DAY OFF?!
AW MAN!

SORRY, GANG. THE CHIEF WANTS COFFEE.
BZZZ
THE CHIEF?
JIMMY'S BOSS. MR. WHITE.
OKAY. WE'LL CATCH UP WITH YOU LATER.
OKAY.
SEE YA.
TEXT
TEXT
TEXT
CRASH!
SUPERMAN FAMILY ADVENTURES

CLICK
CLICK
CRACK!
SMASH!
CRACK!
YAAAARRGH!

YYAARRGHH!
!
HUH?
SUPERMAN?
YYESSS...
AAHHHHHH!!
AAHH!
AAAHHH!!!
MEANWHILE, INSIDE THE FORTRESS OF SOLITUDE...
TAP TAP
PRESS
PRESS
CRUNCH

AAAHH!!
SUPERBOY, DID YOU HEAR THAT CRY FOR HELP?
YEAH. SOUNDED LIKE JIMMY.
COMING FROM METROPOLIS?
YEP.
I'M GONNA GO CHECK IT OUT!
YOUR SUPER HEARING WORKS GREAT!
THANKS, STAR.
AW YEAH TITANS! I'LL BE BACK LATER!
WHERE'S SUPERGIRL GOING?
METROPOLIS.
YOU KNOW US SUPERHEROES, ALWAYS OFF SAVING THE WORLD.
TRUE STORY.
BYE!

YAAHG!
STOMP
STOMP
HELP!
WHAT'S GOING ON DOWN THERE?!
YYAARG!
HUH?
SUPER ZARRO-GIRL?
ME AM COUSIN!
MY COUSIN?
YES! WE PLAY!
CATCH TRAIN!
AAHH!
CATCH
THANK YOU, SUPERGIRL!
YOU'RE WELCOME.
CATCH METROPOLIS MAN!
AAH!

NICE CATCH! THANK YOU, SUPERGIRL!
YOU'RE WELCOME.
AAHH!!
CATCH METROPOLIS MOTORIST!
THANKS, SUPERGIRL!
YOU'RE WELCOME.
CATCH CAT STUCK IN TREE!
MEEOOWWW!
MEOW WOW WOW MEOW!
CATCH!
MEEOW!
NO MORE PLAYING AROUND!
IT'S TIME TO CALM DOWN!
SORRY FOR THE DELAY, JIMMY. I HAD A FEW DISTRACTIONS.
S'OKAY.
YAARRGGHH!
I HEAR YA, BIG GUY. WHY ARE YOU ACTING SO CRAZY? AND WHY ARE YOU DRESSED LIKE SUPERMAN?!
ME AM SUPERMAN!

BIZARRO SUPERMAN!
STOMP!
BIZARRO SUPERMAN?
HE'S RIGHT, KARA.
ON BIZARRO WORLD HE IS SUPERMAN!
BIZARRO WORLD?
SUPERMAN!
YOU MEAN HE COMES FROM A DIFFERENT UNIVERSE?
YES. AN OPPOSITE UNIVERSE.
WELL, YOU SEE...
SLAP!
WOOSH!
FFFFFSSSHH!!!
WELCOME TO SMALLVILLE
WHAM!
KENT FARM

—AW YEAH DESSERTS!

SUPERMAN
FAMILY ADVENTURES
STREAKY?
STREAKY THE SUPER CAT?!!
WOW! SUCH AN HONOR TO MEET YOU, SIR!
I'M FUZZY THE KRYPTO MOUSE!
I GOT SUPER POWERS FROM KRYPTO THE SUPER DOG!
I CAN FLY!
AND I'M SUPER STRONG!
I CAN SEE THROUGH THINGS, TOO!

THAT'S RIGHT!
I USED TO BE A REGULAR MOUSE...
... GETTING CHASED BY CATS LIKE YOU ALL THE TIME!
BUT NOT ANYMORE!
NOW, I'M SUPER!
SWAT!
FOOSH!
CRASH!
I WOULD HAVE FELT THAT...
...IF I WASN'T A SUPER MOUSE.
OUCH.
-CRASHIN' HERE.

SO, YOU BROUGHT HIM TO THE FORTRESS?
YEAH! ISN'T IT GREAT?! BIZ REALLY LIKES CEREAL!
AQUA-OH'S
SUPERMAN FAMILY ADVENTURES
ME AM LOVE NEW HOME!
ME AM WARM HERE!
UNTHANK YOU VERY LITTLE, KAL-EL!
KAL? HE KNOWS YOUR KRYPTONIAN NAME?
YES. HE THINKS HE IS ME.
HE TALKS BACKWARDS!
YAH! YAH! YAH! YAH! YAH! YAH!
STOMP! STOMP! STOMP
YAH! YA! YAH!
KEEP AN EYE ON HIM, KIDS.
CLARK KENT'S NEEDED BACK IN METROPOLIS!
OH, YEAH. THE DAY JOB.
GOOD LUCK!
ZIP!

BIZARRO?
ACCORDING TO THE MESS...
...HE WENT THAT WAY!
INTO THE DINING ROOM?
DINING ROOM
THE FURNITURE!
IT'S STUCK TO THE CEILING!
EVERYTHING RIGHTSIDE DOWN JUST LIKE BIZARRO WORLD!
SEE MORE!
FOOSH
UH OH, WE'D BETTER CATCH HIM BEFORE HE TURNS EVERYTHING INTO BIZARRO WORLD!
YEAH, I THINK YOU'RE RIGHT.

HELLO, MY SON.
KAL-EL?
DADDY!

HUGS!
BIZARRO?
PA?
NICE TO SEE YOU.
DO YOU LIKE MY NEW SUIT?
THAT AM BAD OUTFIT!
WOOO!!
WHAT A NICE KID.
HI, UNCLE JOR-EL!
HELLO, KARA.
CONNER.
HAVE YOU SEEN A LARGE, WEIRD-LOOKING BACKWARDS SUPERMAN TYPE OF GUY FLY THROUGH HERE?
YEP. HE WENT THAT WAY.
THANK YOU. NICE SUIT.
THANKS.

OH, NO! LOOKS LIKE BIZARRO WENT INTO THE KRYPTONITE ROOM!
KRYPTONITE ROOM
NOPE, NOT GOING IN THERE!
GREEN KRYPTONITE
YELLOW KRYPTONITE
RED KRYPTONITE
BLUE KRYPTONITE
AAHHHH!!!

BIZ JUST SCATTERED DIFFERENT-COLORED KRYPTONITE ALL OVER THE PLACE!
NOT GOOD.
VERY DANGEROUS!
WE MUST COLLECT THEM ALL!
I'LL GET THE ANTI-KRYPTONITE LEAD SUITS!
HUH?
A STAMPEDE?
ALL OUR KRYPTONIAN ANIMAL SPECIES!
RUN
STOMP
TROT
HIKE
BIZARRO LET THEM OUT OF THEIR CAGES!
REALLY?
ALL OF THEM?!
STOMP STOMP
YEP.
THAT'S ALL OF THEM.
BAM
STOMP
STOMP
BAM

SCRATCH THAT!
YOU GET THE LEAD SUITS
I'LL GET THE GIANT PET LEASHES!
RIGHT!
FOOSH! ZIP!
MINIATURE CITY ROOM
HEWWO WIDDLE PEEPLE!
BIZARRO!
GIVE ME THE BOTTLE CITY OF KANDOR, PLEASE.
HERE GO!
THANK YOU.
WHEW!
WOOSH
MAKE SURE WE PICK UP ALL THE KRYPTONITE, KRYPTO!
WE DON'T WANT TO LEAVE ANY!
WOOF!
OPEN THE CAGE!
THERE ARE MORE CREATURES ON THE WAY!
NOW, HOW DO WE GET BIZARRO'S ATTENTION?

I GOT IT!
BE RIGHT BACK!
ZIP!
30 SECONDS LATER...
METROPOLIS ICE CREAM
WHAT THE..?!
SORRY, SIR. I'LL HAVE YOU BACK IN METROPOLIS BY DINNER TIME!
THIS WORKED EARLIER, SO...
...ICE CREAM TREATS FOR EVERYONE!
UM, LOOKS LIKE BIZ IS STAYING FOR SURE, HUH?
METROPOLIS ICE CREAM
MMM! ME AM ICE CREAM TASTY!
DON'T GET TOO COMFY, KIDS... WE STILL HAVE A FEW HUNDRED KRYPTONIAN SPECIES TO GATHER!
AW YEAH SUPER ZOO!

SUPERMAN FAMILY ADVENTURES
DAILY PL
HELLO, JIMMY.
SUPERMAN?
YEP. IT'S REALLY ME THIS TIME.
I HAVE SOMETHING FOR YOU.
A WRIST-WATCH?
A SUPER SIGNAL WATCH!
NEXT TIME YOU'RE IN TROUBLE,
PRESS THE BUTTON...
...AND HELP WILL BE ON THE WAY!
SO, YOU DON'T HAVE TO SCREAM ANYMORE.
COFFEE!
DAILY
IT WON'T HELP WITH MR. WHITE, WILL IT?
YOU'RE ON YOUR OWN THERE, JIMMY.
LATER.
COFFEE!
–YES, SIR!

SUPER-PETS.
WHY ARE YOU FOLLOWING ME?!
ART BALTAZAR 2012!

MEANWHILE, IN THE FAR REACHES OF SPACE...
...A FIERY METEORITE IS ON A COLLISION COURSE TOWARDS EARTH!
MORE IMPORTANT... METROPOLIS!
SEE?!!
THAT'S HOW YOU START A STORY!
WHERE'S OLSEN?!
HERE, CHIEF!
WHERE'S MY...?
COFFEE, CHIEF?
TWO CREAMS. TWO SUGARS.
WHERE ARE THOSE...?
PHOTOS, SIR?

I DON'T KNOW HOW YOU DO IT, OLSEN!
SUPERMAN'S MY PAL, CHIEF.
SUPERMAN FAMILY ADVENTURES
NOT HIM. I'M TALKING ABOUT THE COFFEE!
AND DON'T CALL ME CHIEF!
OKAY.
DRINK
NOW, GO!
GET ME MORE PHOTOS!
RIGHT, CHIEF!

♫
HI, GANG!
HI, JIMMY! WHERE ARE YOU GOING?
ON MY WAY TO GET MORE PHOTOS OF SUPERMAN!
REALLY? THAT'S AWESOME!
HOW DO YOU GET SUCH COOL PHOTOS OF THE MAN OF STEEL?
I KNOW HIM!
NO WAY!
IT'S TRUE. I'M HIS PAL.
EVEN HIS COUSIN SUPERGIRL SAVED ME A FEW TIMES.
REALLY? SHE MUST BE SOME KIND OF GAL!
OH, C'MON! YOU'RE LYING!
NO, I'M NOT. IT'S ALL TRUE.
HE EVEN GAVE ME THIS WATCH TO CALL HIM WHENEVER I'M IN TROUBLE.
OH, YEAH? WHY DON'T YOU CALL HIM NOW?!
I'M NOT IN TROUBLE NOW.

WELL, YOU'RE GONNA BE!
ZZZEEEEEEEEEEEEEEEEEEEEEEE
BEPPO?
EEP EEP EEK OP ORK OP!
EEP EEP!
BOO!
AAAH!!
I DON'T UNDERSTAND...
... SOMETHING'S NOT RIGHT.
IT WAS SUPPOSED TO BE SUPERMAN.
SURE, PAL. I BELIEVE YA.
NEVER KNEW SUPERMAN WAS SO SMALL.
AND CUTE!

LATER, OUTSIDE METROPOLIS HIGH SCHOOL...
OLSEN!
I BET YOU THOUGHT THAT WAS PRETTY FUNNY, HUH?
WELL, ACTUALLY...
HI, JIMMY!
HI, CHLOE. HI, NATASHA.
CLICK!
CLICK!
CLICK!
Y'KNOW, THAT CHLOE SURE LOOKS A LOT LIKE SUPERGIRL, DON'T YOU THINK?
I DON'T CARE, OLSEN!
YOU JUST KEEP YOUR MONKEY AWAY FROM ME!
BEPPO'S NOT MY MONKEY.
YEAH, RIGHT!
I WAS CALLING SUPERMAN AND THE SUPER MONKEY SHOWED UP!
THERE'S GOTTA BE SOMETHING WRONG WITH THIS WATCH!
BOOM!
IT'S AN ALIEN INVASION!
QUICK!
JIMMY!
USE YOUR WATCH TO CALL SUPERMAN!

RIGHT! RIGHT!
ZZZEEEEEEEEEEEEEEEEEEEEEEE
WOOOSHH!
STREAKY?
I DON'T UNDERSTAND.
BOOM!
A GIANT POINTY-HEADED ALIEN MONSTER IS ATTACKING!
I'M ON IT! C'MON, SUPERMAN!
ZZZEEEEEEEEEEEEEEE
COMET?
THE SUPER HORSE?
AAAHHH!!!

A GIANT SLIMY SIX-EYED ALIEN MONSTER WITH TENTACLES!
KRYPTO?
HIYA, JIMMY!
FUZZY?
DON'T WORRY. THE WATCH IS WORKING.

YOUR MONKEY IS RIGHT HERE.
HE'S NOT MY MONKEY.
I THINK HE LIKES YOU.
WHOOOO
WHOOOOOOOOSSHH!
YYAAYY!!
JIMMY?
YES, SIR?

SORRY ABOUT THAT LITTLE MIX-UP! SEEMS I GAVE YOU THE SUPER PETS WATCH BY MISTAKE.
S'OKAY.
HERE'S THE RIGHT ONE. CALL ANYTIME YOU NEED TO.
THANK YOU, SIR.
WOW! YOU REALLY DO KNOW SUPERMAN!
TOLD YA.
YOU GOT ONE OF THOSE WATCHES THAT CALLS SUPERGIRL?
THAT WOULD BE NICE.
HOW ABOUT ONE THAT CALLS JIMMY OLSEN?
I'D WEAR TWO OF THOSE!
AAHHH!!
LEAVE ME ALONE, MONKEY!
-WHAT TIME IS IT?

COOL!
THE WAY US SUPER PETS WORKED TOGETHER WITH OUR SUPER BREATH!
BLEW THOSE ALIENS AWAY, WE DID!
TRUE.
SUPERMAN
FAMILY
NOW WE MUST CONTINUE YOUR SUPER TRAINING!
LET'S START WITH X-RAY VISION!
OKAY!
SORRY.
S'OKAY. HAPPENS ALL THE TIME.
ANYWAY, LET'S MOVE TO THE KITCHEN FOR HEAT VISION TRAINING.
WE MUST USE PRECISE CONTROL. TAKES LOTS OF CONCENTRATION!
POP POP
POP POP
NICE!

ANY MISCALCULATION COULD HAVE DRASTIC, DEVASTATING RESULTS.
REALLY? LIKE WHAT?
LET'S JUST SAY, MY SUPER TRAINING DIDN'T GO SO GOOD.
SHOW 'EM THE SHORTS, KRYPTO!
IT'S ALL ABOUT CONTROL.
WOW. THAT EXPLAINS A LOT!
NOW YA KNOW WHY KAL NEEDED A NEW SUIT! HA!
—THE HOLE TRUTH.

SUPERMAN FAMILY ADVENTURES
DID YOU SEE THE WAY THE SUPER PETS SENT THOSE ALIENS BACK INTO SPACE THIS MORNING?
UM, NO, ACTUALLY. I MISSED IT. WAS SUPERMAN THERE?
HE SURE WAS. HE SWOOPED IN, GAVE JIMMY SOMETHING, THEN FLEW AWAY WITH THE PETS.
YEAH, I HOPE THAT WATCH WORKS THIS TIME.
HUH?
HOW DO YOU KNOW SUPERMAN GAVE JIMMY A WATCH?
YOU JUST SAID YOU WEREN'T THERE.
UM... JUST LUCKY, I GUESS.
HHMM.
YOU ARE VERY STRANGE SOMETIMES, KENT.
I THINK YOU KNOW MORE ABOUT SUPERMAN THAN YOU ARE TELLING ME.
LIKE, WHERE WERE YOU WHEN THE SUPER PETS STOPPED THE ALIENS?
I WAS EATING BREAKFAST, LOIS.
OH, YEAH? WHAT ABOUT WHEN BIZARRO RAMPAGED THROUGH METROPOLIS?

BYE.
I WAS VISITING MY MOM AT THE KENT FARM.
HMM... WHAT ABOUT WHEN THOSE LEX-BOTS WERE IN TOWN?
FALL!
BAM!
PUNCH!
FIGHT!
SKYDIVING!
SKYDIVING? C'MON, CLARK.
LIKE I SAID, YOU ARE A STRANGE ONE, SMALLVILLE.
HOW ABOUT A SNACK?
HELLO, SIR. TWO COTTON CANDIES, PLEASE.
WOULD YOU LIKE PINK OR BLUE, CLARK?
I LIKE PINK VERY MUCH, LOIS.

WHAT?
THAT'S WHAT SUPERMAN SAYS.
UM... REALLY?
♫
BBZZZZ
MEANWHILE, AT THE FORTRESS OF SOLITUDE...
BBZ BZZZ
KARA! OPERATION PINK!
PINK!
NOW WHICH CRYSTAL?
OH, THE PINK ONE! RIGHT!
NOW TO DEPLOY...

... THE SUPERMAN ROBOT!
WHAT HAPPENED HERE?
OPERATION PINK!
OH, IT'S THE PINK CRYSTAL.
KARA!
WAIT!
NO!
BMMMM!
FOOOOSSSHH!
UH, OH. NOW THERE ARE TWO OF THEM HEADING TO METROPOLIS.
UM... NOT GOOD.

SO, ANYWAY...
ENOUGH PLAYING AROUND! TELL ME WHAT YOU KNOW ABOUT SUPERMAN!
WELL, Y'SEE...
SWOOOSH!
SUPERMAN?
WOW!
LOOK AT THAT, LOIS!
ME AND SUPERMAN BOTH HERE AT THE SAME TIME!
YES.
QUITE ODD INDEED.

SUPERMAN, HOW ABOUT AN INTERVIEW FOR THE DAILY PLANET?
SURE, MISS LANE!
THIS LOOKS LIKE A JOB...
...FOR SUPERMAN!
TWO SUPERMEN?
HOW?
WHO IS...?
YES!
AW BOY.
I AM THE REAL SUPERMAN!
LOOK! I AM REALLY STRONG!
ME, TOO!
SSHHHH

HEY!
AW YEAH
HOT DOGS!
I CAN LIFT HEAVY THINGS!
ME, TOO!
HEY!
CAN THROW THEM, TOO!
HEY!
AW YEAH
HOT DOGS
ME, TOO!
HEY!
UH, OH.
SWOOSH!
THANK YOU, ANOTHER SUPERMAN?
CATCH!
GRAB!

CLARK.
FOOSHH!
CLARK, ARE YOU SEEING THIS?
OH, GEE, LOIS.
SURE IS SWELL!
SWELL?
THERE ARE THREE SUPERMEN AND YOU SAY "SWELL"?
BBZZZ
BESIDES, LOIS, I ONLY SEE ONE SUPERMAN.
FOOSH!
MAYBE NOW'S A GOOD TIME FOR THAT INTERVIEW.
GOOD EVENING, MISS LANE!
I'M FROM KRYPTON!
CAN'T SEE THROUGH LEAD!
RING RING
SOMETHING'S NOT RIGHT HERE, KENT.
YOU'RE ACTING STRANGER THAN NORMAL.

EXCUSE ME, LOIS.
I HAVE TO TAKE THIS.
KARA
WHAT'S UP?
MALFUNCTION?
WHAT DO YOU MEAN?
HOW MANY?
UM, CLARK... YOU MAY WANT TO SEE THIS.
GOLLY GEE, LOIS.
GOLLY GEE, LOIS.
GOLLY GEE, LOIS.
GOLLY GEE, LOIS.
I... UM... BUT... MAYBE...
SAVE IT, SMALLVILLE!
I DON'T EVEN WANT TO KNOW!
TIME FOR ORANGE JUICE!
FRESHLY SQUEEZED?
ZIP IT, CLARK!
OKAY.

-SILENCE? YES.

TITANO?!
EEP!
CLICK!
COFFEE!!
IT'S A
MONKEY
METROPOLIS!
ART BALTAZAR 2012!

MEANWHILE, IN THE FAR REACHES OF SPACE...
A RED KRYPTONITE METEORITE IS ON A COLLISION COURSE WITH EARTH!
BUT MORE IMPORTANT...
METROPOLIS!
ANOTHER METEORITE?
FALLING FROM THE SKY?
HOW?
WHY?
LET'S BACKTRACK TEN MINUTES...
TEN MINUTES AGO...
...AT THE FORTRESS OF SOLITUDE...
BIZARRO!
COME ON, BIZARRO!
IT'S TIME FOR YOUR WALK!

SUPERMAN
FAMILY ADVENTURES
ME AM NOT READY!
ME AM LIKE NOT EXERCISE!
HERE WE GO.
CLICK!
WHOO HOOOO!!

EERT!
WHAT? WHAT IS IT, BIZARRO?
RED?
RED! RED KRYPTONITE! VERY BAD!

OH NO. I MUST HAVE MISSED THAT ONE WHEN I CLEANED UP.
THROW FAR AWAY!
YES!
THROW!
WOOSH!
TEN MINUTES LATER...
...AT THE DAILY PLANET...

SIP
OLSEN!
WHERE'S MY COFFEE?
THERE'S NOTHING HERE BUT AN EMPTY CUP!
WHY DO I PAY YOU, OLSEN?!
I WANT A NEW CUP OF COFFEE WAITING ON MY DESK WHEN I GET BACK!

DAILY PLANET
CRASH!
PLUNK
SIP
GULP
SWALLOW!
TITANO!
THERE YOU ARE.

WHO'S YOUR FRIEND, LOIS?
OH, HI, CLARK. MEET TITANO.
HE'S VISITING FROM HALEY'S CIRCUS TO DO A COVER PHOTOSHOOT FOR THE DAILY PLANET!
THAT'S GREAT! HELLO, TITANO.
WHO'S YOUR FRIEND, CLARK?
HUH?
OH, THAT'S BOB! BOB KENT. MY PET MONKEY!
SO, BOB LOOKS A LITTLE NEAR-SIGHTED, HUH?
WELL, YOU KNOW US KENTS.
RIGHT.
SO. I CAN ASSUME YOUR MONKEY HAILS FROM THE SAME GALAXY AS YOU DO?
UM, GALAXY, LOIS?
SMALLVILLE, CLARK.
OH, RIGHT! THE SMALLVILLE GALAXY!
STRAIGHT FROM THE KENT FARM!
MONKEYS ON A FARM, KENT?
YEAH, OKAY. WHATEVER.
YOU'RE A STRANGE ONE, CLARK.

UM, LOIS?
IS TITANO SUPPOSED TO GLOW?
WHAT?
EEP!
LEAP
JUMP
JUMP
FALL
SHAKE
SHAKE
SHAKE
THOOM!

HMM... THAT'S SOME STRONG COFFEE.
UH, GEE, LOIS! I JUST REMEMBERED...
...I LEFT MY KITCHEN LIGHT ON!
SWOOSH!
DON'T YOU HAVE TO GO, TOO?
EEP!
SWOOSH!

TITANO! CALM DOWN, BIG FELLA!
EVERYTHING WILL BE OKAY!
GRAB!
ULK!
UM... HELLO THERE.
LEAP!
DAILY PLANET
NET
SO, UM... WHAT'S ON YOUR MIND, BIG GUY?

SQUEEZE
SQUEEZE
TAP
TAP
OOK?
EEP!
OOK! OOK!
OOK! OOK!
EEP! EEP! EEP! EEP!
OOK! OOK!
OOK! EEP! EEP!
OOKLA!
NOW! WHILE HE'S DISTRACTED!
MAYBE I CAN TALK SOME SENSE INTO HIM!

TITANO! I'M HERE TO HELP YOU!
NO NEED TO BE ANGRY!
ZAP!
FALL!
BAM!
UGH!
SO... WEIRD!
I'M... FEELING...
...EFFECTS ...OF...
...RED KRYPTONITE?
HOW CAN THAT BE?
MAYBE TITANO HAS BEEN EXPOSED SOMEHOW!
THE EFFECTS ARE SO UNPREDICTABLE!
I NEVER KNOW...
... WHAT WILL HAPPEN.
WHAT?!
THAT'S RIGHT, KAL-EL!
THAT RED KRYPTONITE RELEASED YOUR DARK SIDE!
CALL ME... THE NEGATIVE SUPERMAN!

NOW, GET LOST!
I'LL SHOW YOU HOW TO HANDLE A GIANT MONKEY!
ACTUALLY, HE'S AN APE.
SHADDUP, KENT!
LANE! UPDATE!
TITANO STARTED TO GLOW RED.
THEN HE TURNED INTO A GIANT APE.
THEN, SUPERMAN GOT ZAPPED AND HE SPLIT INTO TWO PEOPLE.
HA! ONLY IN METROPOLIS!
OLSEN!
DRINK
CLICK
CLICK
DAILY PLANET
OOK.
OOK. OOK.
EEP.
EEP. EEP.
OOK. OOK.
EEP. EEP.
OOK. OOK.

TITANO! I AM NOT HERE TO HELP YOU!
DON'T LISTEN TO HIM, TITANO!
GREAT KRYPTON! YOU ARE SO NEGATIVE!
THIS IS TRUE.
Y'SEE...
... WE ARE NEGATIVE FROM EACH OTHER.
LIKE A MAGNET.
I CAN REPEL YOU EVER SO SLIGHTLY.
HEY!
GRAB!
CLOSE ENOUGH FOR THE SCARY GIANT APE TO GET YA!
WELL, TIME TO GO TO WORK!

WORK?
OH, DON'T WORRY. I WON'T DO A GOOD JOB.
YOU'LL BE FIRED BY THE END OF THE DAY.
SEE YA!
SWOOSH
RARGHHR!
THROW!
WOW. THIS NEWS DAY IS JUST FLYING BY.
CLICK
CLICK
WOOSH!

AHEM!
KENT?
CAN'T?
KANT.
CLARK KANT.
KANT.
CLICK
CLICK
AS IN, CLARK KANT CAN'T DO IT.
NO WAY! NOT GONNA.
WOW, YOU ARE SO NEGATIVE.
IT'S WHO I AM, LOIS.
IT'S WHO I AM.
I DON'T LIKE IT.
WHERE'S THE REAL CLARK?
I DON'T KNOW AND I DON'T CARE.
MR. KANT?
WOULD YOU CARE TO STEP OUTSIDE?
PFFT!
CLICK
CLICK
NOPE.
YOU KNOW I CAN'T DO THAT.

GRAB
GRAB
FFSSH!
WWOOSSSH!!
WHAT'S GOING ON HERE, LANE?
I THINK WE'RE ABOUT TO FIND OUT.
YAHGAH RAHGH!!
RARGH YAHHR!!

SHAKE SHAKE
SHAKE SHAKE
SMASH!
UNGH! I THINK TITANO JUST SMASHED US BACK TOGETHER.
YOU HAVEN'T HEARD THE LAST OF ME!
SHAKE SHAKE
SHAKE SHAKE
OOK?
DINK DING DINK
EEWWW!
CLICK CLICK CLICK

SHRINK
FALL
CATCH
TITANO!
YOU'RE OKAY!
BEPPO!
YOU'RE A HERO!
OLSEN!
GET THAT MONKEY TO HIS PHOTOSHOOT!
RIGHT, CHIEF!
AND DON'T CALL ME MONKEY!
RIGHT, MONK... UM... CHIEF.
I MEAN CHIEF!

-HE'S BACK?! WHAT DOES THIS MEAN? ONLY TIME WILL TELL!

SUPERMAN?! WHAT ARE YOU DOING?
PINK1
WAIT! LOIS! THAT'S NOT ME!
WHO IS THE PURPLE SUPERMAN?!
ART BALTAZAR 2012

MEANWHILE, IN THE FAR REACHES OF SPACE...
A MYSTERIOUS RADIOACTIVE PURPLE METEORITE IS ON A COLLISION COURSE WITH EARTH!
BUT MORE IMPORTANT...
...METROPOLIS!
WHEN SUDDENLY...
GRAB!
YOINK!
WWSSH!

SUPERMAN FAMILY ADVENTURES
LOOK! MR. LUTHOR! IT'S A LITTLE BITTY ONE!
OTIS! DISCARD THIS PUNY ROCK!
MISS TESCHMACHER...
...DON'T STOP SEARCHING THE SKIES UNTIL WE FIND A ROCK LIKE THIS KRYPTONITE!
RED
...SUPERMAN'S WEAKNESS IS OUT THERE SOMEWHERE!
HMM... SURE IS SHINY...
...AND OH SO PURPLE!

I'M KEEPING IT!
WELL, WHADDAYA KNOW?!
IT'S TIME FOR LUNCH!
MEANWHILE, IN THE DAILY PLANET BREAKROOM...
MMMMM
TING!
HI, JIMMY!
YIKES!
GOSH, MR. KENT!
YOU STARTLED ME!
MR. KENT! THAT'S SCALDING HOT! HOW ARE YOU...?
OH, RIGHT.
OUCH.

MEANWHILE, ON THE STREETS OF METROPOLIS...
ONE CHOCOLATE BAR, PLEASE.
OTIS? YOU'RE PURPLE?
WELL, HOW 'BOUT THAT?!
HERE'S YOUR DAILY CANDY.
CHOCO
OH, SO SLEEPY...
TOUCH!
OOPS. SORRY ABOUT THAT!
ZZZZZ.
HMM... I HOPE HE FEELS BETTER.
I, ON THE OTHER HAND, FEEL GREAT!
LIKE I JUST GOT SOME EXTRA STRENGTH!
MUST BE SOMETHING IN THE CHOCOLATE.

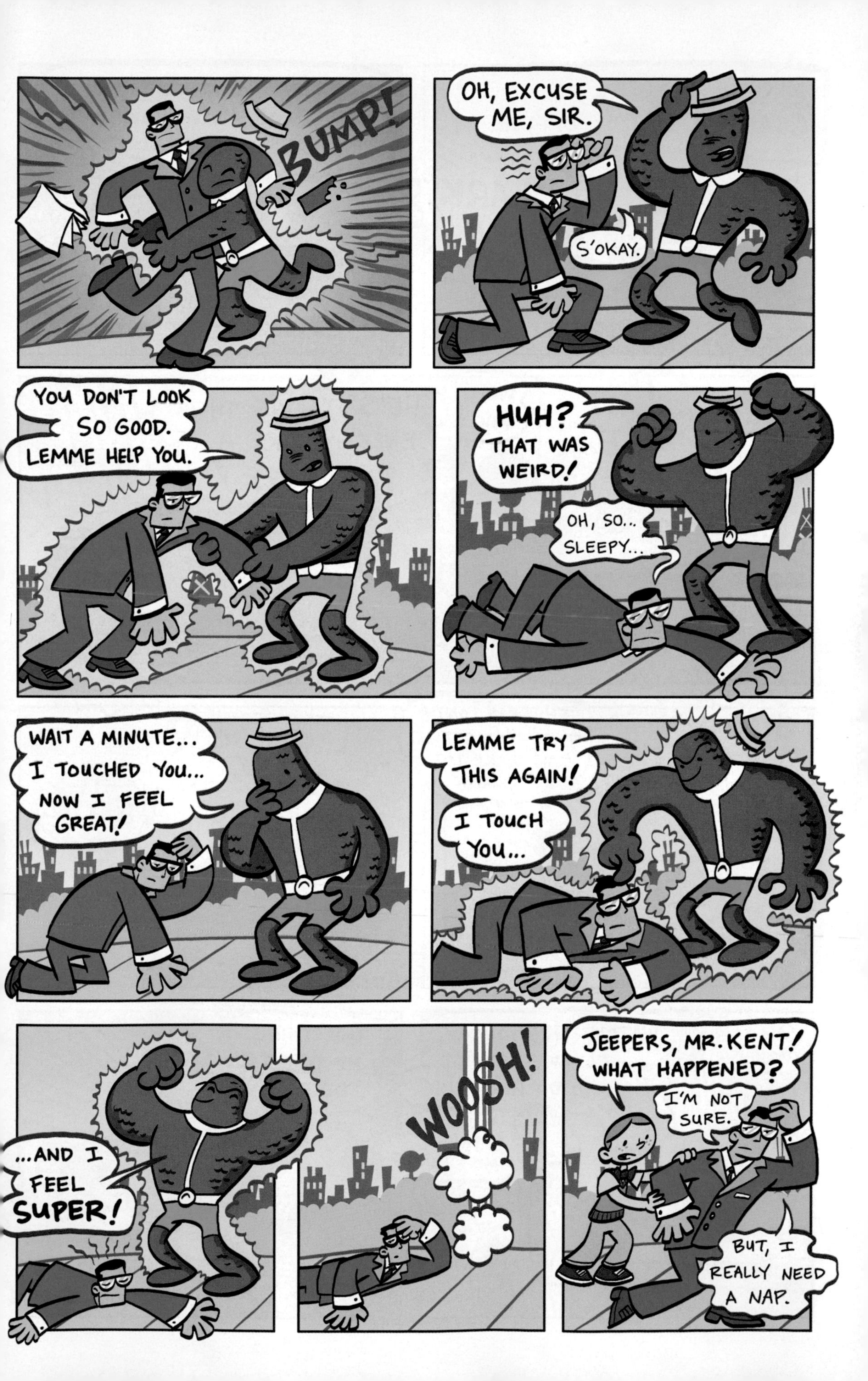
BUMP!
OH, EXCUSE ME, SIR.
S'OKAY.
YOU DON'T LOOK SO GOOD. LEMME HELP YOU.
HUH? THAT WAS WEIRD!
OH, SO... SLEEPY...
WAIT A MINUTE... I TOUCHED YOU... NOW I FEEL GREAT!
LEMME TRY THIS AGAIN!
I TOUCH YOU...
...AND I FEEL SUPER!
WOOSH!
JEEPERS, MR. KENT! WHAT HAPPENED?
I'M NOT SURE.
BUT, I REALLY NEED A NAP.

MINUTES LATER, IN CLARK KENT'S OFFICE...
CLARK, WAKE UP!
SOMEONE IS MAKING THE PEOPLE OF METROPOLIS FALL ASLEEP!
YAWN!
HE'S TAKING THEIR ENERGY LIKE A... PARASITE!
ZZZZ.
ZZZZ.
ZZZZ.
JIMMY!
THERE'S ONLY ONE THING THAT CAN WAKE UP CLARK.
YES, MISS LANE?
ZZZZ.
RIGHT! THE CHIEF'S COFFEE!
SIP SIP SIP
ZOOP!
WATCH THIS, JIMMY. CLARK'S ABOUT TO DO HIS THING.
WHAT THING, MISS LANE?
THE THING HE DOES BEST!
THIS LOOKS LIKE A JOB FOR...

HA HA HEE HOH!
HEY, MAN! STOP STEALING PEOPLE'S ENERGY!
IT FEELS SO GOOD!
IT'S YOU!
I SENSE MUCH STRENGTH IN YOU!
I NEED MORE SUPER ENERGY!
AAHGR!!
THIS PARASITE IS DRAINING MY POWERS!
HA! I AM SUPER ONCE AGAIN!
SO... SLEEPY...
NOW, I WILL BE THE NEW HERO OF METROPOLIS!
YAWN.

NIGHTY NIGHT, SUPES!
TRY SOME COFFEE, SUPERMAN!
IT WILL WAKE YOU UP! I'VE SEEN IT HAPPEN BEFORE!
SIP
ZING!
WOW! WHAT'S IN THAT STUFF?
ATTENTION, SLEEPY PEOPLE OF METROPOLIS!
ZZZZ.
ZZZZ.
ZZZZ.
I AM YOUR SAVIOR! I AM THE PURPLE SUPERMAN!
ZZZZ.
PURPLE SUPERMAN? REALLY? THAT'S WHAT YOU CAME UP WITH?
ZZZZ.
ZZZZ.
I LIKE WHAT YOU CALLED HIM EARLIER... PARASITE!
MISS LANE?
YOU SEEM TO HAVE ALL THE ABILITIES SUPERMAN HAS.
OH, MY GOODNESS! YOU ARE BEAUTIFUL!
AND APPARENTLY HIS FEELINGS, TOO.

RACE YA?
HUH?
YOU!
I HAVE ALL YOUR POWERS!
REALLY?
BUT FOR HOW LONG?
LONG ENOUGH TO BEAT YOU IN A RACE!
COOL. LET'S GO!
SWOOSH!
INTERESTING. LOOKS LIKE SUPERMAN WAS WEARING OVEN MITTS?
YEP. I'M GUESSING IT'S ALL PART OF HIS PLAN, MISS LANE.
CLICK
CLICK
SNAP

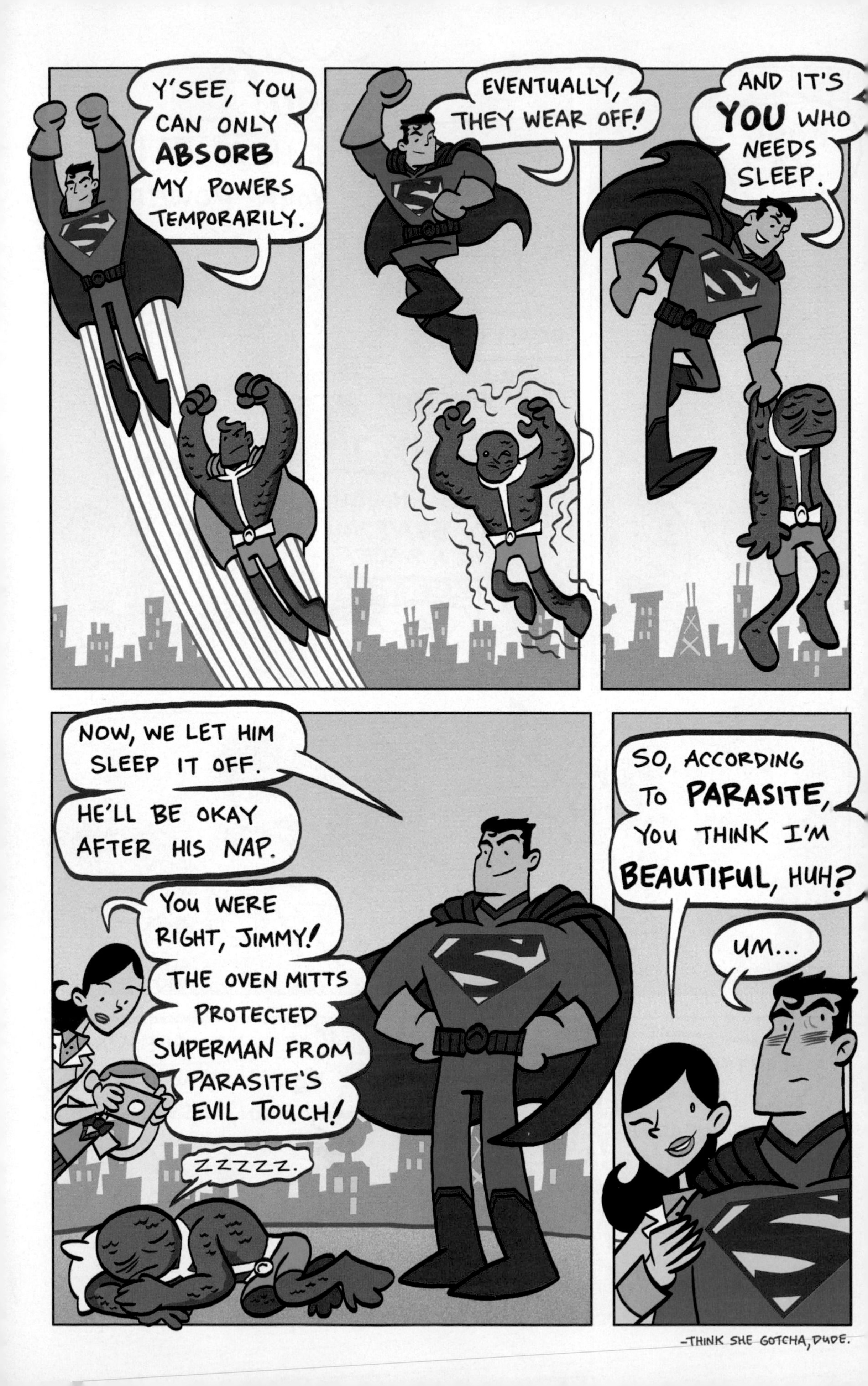
Y'SEE, YOU CAN ONLY ABSORB MY POWERS TEMPORARILY.
EVENTUALLY, THEY WEAR OFF!
AND IT'S YOU WHO NEEDS SLEEP.
NOW, WE LET HIM SLEEP IT OFF.
HE'LL BE OKAY AFTER HIS NAP.
YOU WERE RIGHT, JIMMY!
THE OVEN MITTS PROTECTED SUPERMAN FROM PARASITE'S EVIL TOUCH!
ZZZZZ.
SO, ACCORDING TO PARASITE, YOU THINK I'M BEAUTIFUL, HUH?
UM...
-THINK SHE GOTCHA, DUDE.

SPECIAL DELIVERY!
TO: THE SUPER PETS
THIS SIDE UP
THUMP!
SUPERMAN FAMILY ADVENTURES
SUPER-PETS! CHECK THIS OUT!
WHAT IS IT?
CAN WE OPEN IT?
OF COURSE! IT'S ADDRESSED TO US!
OH, BOY! A BOX OF DOGGIE TREATS!
AND... CHEESE LOGS!
NICE!

THIS SIDE UP
THIS SIDE UP
THIS SIDE UP
THMP!
THIS SIDE UP
A FLOATING SUPERMAN ACTION FIGURE?
THIS SIDE UP
DID YOU DO THAT?
DO WHAT?
THIS SIDE UP
NOTHING!
I NEED MORE SLEEP.
THIS SIDE UP
-FULLY POSABLE.

SUPERMAN FAMILY ADVENTURES
SO, LEX LUTHOR. YOU WANT TO BE OUR NEW DAILY PLANET INTERN?
YES.
SAYS YOU HAVE EXPERIENCE AS AN EVIL GENIUS.
THAT'S CORRECT.
IT SAYS HERE... YOU ARE THE "GREATEST CRIMINAL MIND OF OUR TIME."
SO TRUE.
I CAN'T HIRE YOU!
YOU TRIED TO DESTROY THE CITY WITH ROBOTS!
ONLY ONCE.
LOOK! IS THAT SUPERMAN?!
WHERE?
STAMP!
WELL, LOOK AT THAT...
...LOOKS LIKE YOU'VE BEEN APPROVED!
MUST HAVE OVERLOOKED IT.
APPROVED!

WELCOME TO THE DAILY PLANET, THE GREATEST NEWSPAPER OF METROPOLIS!
ROVED!
I'M REALLY LOOKING FORWARD TO YOUR COMPUTER FILES ON THE SUPERMAN FAMILY.
NO TIME FOR THAT. FIRST ORDER OF BUSINESS... COFFEE!
OLSEN!
APPROVED!
YES, CHIEF?
SHOW MR. LUTHOR THE BEST WAY TO MAKE A FRESH CUP OF COFFEE.
OKAY, CHIEF.
AND DON'T CALL ME CHIEF!
SECONDS LATER...
POUR
TWO CREAMS...
AW YEAH SWEETENER
AW YEAH SWEETENER
... TWO SUGARS.
JUST THE WAY THE CHIEF LIKES IT.
NONSENSE. YOU CALL THAT COFFEE?
CHIEF DOES.
HOLD ON. I'LL BE RIGHT BACK!
FANCY COFFEE
NOW THIS IS COFFEE!

OLSEN!
GET IN HERE!
HERE YOU GO, CHIEF.
TRY THIS NEW PERUVIAN ITALIAN ROASTED CAPPUCCINO BLEND.
SIP SIP
SPIT!
WHAT DO YOU CALL THIS MESS?!
OLSEN!
SIP.
YOU'RE ON THIN ICE, LUTHOR!
GO DOWNTOWN AND GET PHOTOS!
BOOM!
DAILY PL
SIDEKICK CITY ELEMENTARY
THE SUPER FAMILY IS RESCUING A SCHOOL BUS FROM A VOLCANIC EXPLOSION!

GO!
I DON'T UNDERSTAND! THAT COFFEE WAS TOP-OF-THE-LINE!
CHIEF'S GOT OLD-FASHIONED TASTES!
YOU'LL BE SAFE HERE, KIDS!
THANKS, SUPERBOY!
THANKS, SUPERGIRL!
YOU'RE WELCOME!
SIDEKICK CITY ELEMENTARY
A VOLCANO IN THE MIDDLE OF METROPOLIS? VERY STRANGE.
THIS BOULDER SHOULD PLUG UP THE VOLCANO!
NOW TO COOL OFF THE **LAVA** WITH A LITTLE **FREEZE BREATH**!

THIS IS GOOD STUFF! FRONT PAGE HEADLINES FOR SURE!
NOW'S MY CHANCE TO SLIP AWAY.
A MOMENT LATER...
FINALLY!
ALONE WITH LOIS LANE'S COMPUTER.
THERE'S NO TELLING WHAT SECRETS HER COMPUTER FILES WILL REVEAL OF THAT ALIEN SUPERMAN!
LUTHOR!
GOOD GOSH! HOW MUCH COFFEE CAN ONE MAN DRINK?
NO COFFEE THIS TIME, INTERN.
TOSS
GO WITH LOIS AND TAKE PHOTOS!
C'MON, HURRY!
HURRY!
THE SUPER FAMILY IS SAVING A SINKING OCEAN LINER!

CLICK CLICK CLICK
NOT AS EASY AS YOU THOUGHT, HUH?
WHAT'S THIS? NOW? HE WANTS COFFEE... NOW?
CAN'T OLSEN DO THIS?
BBZZZ
NOPE. JIMMY'S BUSY. IT'S YOUR JOB.
HERE YOU GO!
YOU HAVE COFFEE ON THE HELICOPTER?
WITH MR. WHITE, THERE IS COFFEE EVERYWHERE!
SPECIAL DELIVERY!
AAH!
PUSH
CAREFUL NOT TO SPILL IT!
CONTENTS MAY BE HOT!

Daily Planet
OPEN
IT'S ABOUT TIME!
SWIPE
AARRGHH!!!
I QUIT! I QUIT! I QUIT! I QUIT! I QUIT! I QUIT!
WHAT'S WRONG WITH LUTHOR, CHIEF?
SOUNDS LIKE HE JUST QUIT!
NEED SOME HELP GETTING DOWN, LEX?
YOU!

HOW HUMILIATING!
CURSE YOU, SUPERMAN!
TAKING OVER THE WORLD SHOULD BE MUCH EASIER THAN THIS!
SNAP
CLICK
SNAP
LATER...
GREAT SCOTT! WHAT A DAY!
CAN'T WAIT TO...
PERRY WHITE EDITOR -IN- CHIEF
...WHAT THE..? PURPLE?
WHO ARE YOU?! GET OUT OF MY OFFICE!
RUN RUN!
THE NERVE OF THAT GUY!
BUT I HAVE TO ADMIT...
...HE'S DARN GOOD-LOOKING!
-RHYMES WITH PURPLE.

YOU ARE DEFEATED, SUPERMAN!
NOTHING CAN SAVE YOU NOW!
ART BALTAZAR 2012
THE MENACE OF METALLO!

MEANWHILE IN THE FAR REACHES OF SPACE...
A FIERY ROCKETSHIP IS ON A COLLISION COURSE WITH EARTH!
...BUT MORE IMPORTANT... METROPOLIS!
UNTIL...
CATCH
STOP
GRAB

GOOD JOB, COUSINS!
NICE CATCH, KRYPTO!
SUPERMAN FAMILY ADVENTURES
WOOF!
Daily Planet
HERE YOU GO, CAPTAIN CORBEN!
ALL SAFE AND SOUND!
UM... THANKS, SUPERMAN.
YOU'RE WELCOME, CAPTAIN!
BUT... UM... I DON'T FEEL SO GOOD.

GOOD EVENING! THIS IS LOIS LANE STREAMING LIVE ON THE DAILY PLANET NEWS WEBSITE!
IF YOU'RE JUST JOINING US...
...THE SUPER FAMILY HAS RESCUED ASTRONAUT CAPTAIN JACK CORBEN FROM CRASH-LANDING INTO THE METROPOLIS SEAPORT!
Daily Planet
CAPTAIN CORBEN, WOULD YOU LIKE TO SAY A FEW WORDS?
OH, I... FEEL A...BIT... WOOZY!
FALL
GENTLEMEN! IS THAT MAN ALL RIGHT?!
YEAH! HE WILL BE SOON!
ACCORDING TO THE NAVIGATIONAL READINGS ON THE SHIP, YOU PASSED THROUGH A KRYPTONITE ASTEROID FIELD!
I THINK I GOT THE SPACE SICKNESS!
OOH... UUHNNG...
KRYPTONITE?! WE'D BETTER KEEP AN EYE ON CAPTAIN CORBEN!
LET'S GET THE SHIP TO STAR LABS FOR FURTHER ANALYSIS!

MOMENTS LATER AT STAR LABS...
DOCTOR JOHN HENRY IRONS CONTINUES HIS RESEARCH...
WELL, SUPERMAN, AFTER ANALYZING THE DATA...
...CAPTAIN CORBEN'S SHIP HAS BEEN FUSED WITH...
...AN ALIEN TECHNOLOGY BEYOND ANYTHING FROM THIS EARTH!
REALLY? HOW IS THAT POSSIBLE?!
NOT SURE WHY, BUT THIS SYMBOL KEEPS SHOWING UP.
HHMM. THAT'S THE SAME SYMBOL ON THE LUTHOR SUIT!
INTERESTING.
BUT WHAT'S THE CONNECTION?
I DON'T KNOW.
I'LL CONTINUE MY RESEARCH.
THANK YOU, JOHN.

MEANWHILE, AT THE METROPOLIS HOSPITAL...
OOUUNGHH!
HOW DO YOU FEEL?
LOUSY!
AH YES, OF COURSE...
...THAT'S WHAT HAPPENS WHEN YOU HAVE...
...KRYPTONITE POISONING!
POISONING?
YEP! POISONED FROM RADIOACTIVE PIECES OF SUPERMAN'S HOME PLANET!
SUPERMAN?
YES. IT'S HIS FAULT YOU FEEL SO SICK.
SUPERMAN'S FAULT?

CORRECT!
YOUR BODY IS TURNING INTO HUMAN KRYPTONITE BECAUSE OF SUPERMAN!
!!!
OH, NO! THIS IS TERRIBLE!
AND SUPERMAN IS TO BLAME!
WAIT A MINUTE!
ARE YOU A DOCTOR?
NOT QUITE.
DEAR BOY...
I AM LEX LUTHOR!
EVIL GENIUS AND EXPERT ON THAT ALIEN SUPERMAN!
...AND I HAVE THE ABILITY TO SAVE YOU!
-TO BE CONTINUED...

MEANWHILE, AT THE FORTRESS OF SOLITUDE...
SUPERMAN FAMILY ADVENTURES
HEY, KRYPTO!
WHAT ARE YOU DOING?
WAITING.
WAITING FOR WHAT?
WAITING FOR THE SUPERMOBILE TO MOVE.
WHY?
WHEN IT MOVES, I'M GONNA CHASE IT!
WHY?
I'M A DOG. THAT'S WHAT WE DO.

CHASING CARS?
YEP!
I'M A SUPER DOG! I CHASE SUPER CARS!
UM... KRYPTO...
IT'S NOT MOVING.
IT'S GONNA!
I'LL BE IN THE KITCHEN.
-AW YEAH ANTICIPATION!

DID YOU SEE HOW THE SUPER FAMILY SAVED CAPTAIN CORBEN?!
YEP! I WAS THERE BROADCASTING WITH MISS LANE.
SUPERMAN FAMILY ADVENTURES
I WAS THERE, TOO!
YEAH. I THINK I SAW YOU.
SO, THE NEWS SAID HIS SHIP WAS PART ALIEN?
HOW'S THAT WORK?
THUD!
YOU!
YOU ARE THE ONE WHO KNOWS SUPERMAN!
BRING HIM TO ME... NOW!
EEEEEEEEEEEEEEEEEEEEEEEEE
PRESS

WHAT IS IT, JIMMY?
S'UP?
WOW, THAT WAS FAST!
SO, WHAT CAN I HELP YOU WITH?
I HAVE SOMETHING FOR YOU, SUPERMAN!
OPEN
AAARGH!

THAT'S KRYPTONITE YOU'RE FEELING, SUPERMAN!
AARRGH!
Y'SEE, THAT KRYPTONITE ASTEROID FIELD TURNED MY BODY INTO HUMAN KRYPTONITE!
AND IT'S ALL YOUR FAULT!
THIS LEAD SUIT HELPS ME CONTAIN AND CONTROL MY POWERS!
WHY... ARE... YOU DOING THIS? WHO ARE YOU?
JACK CORBEN?!
YES! THAT WAS MY NAME ONCE!
NOW YOU CAN CALL ME...
...METALLO!

HEY, METALLO!
LEAVE OUR COUSIN ALONE!
REALLY?
BAH! TAKE THAT, MEDDLING KIDS!
WATCH OUT!
WHILE AT STAR LABS...
STAR★LABS
UNCLE JOHN!
THE SUPER FAMILY IS IN TROUBLE!
WHAT?!
THAT CRAZY SPACEMAN IS HURTING THEM WITH KRYPTONITE!
RIGHT! OUR FRIENDS NEED OUR HELP!
SMASH!
UM... UNCLE JOHN... YOU MIGHT NEED SOMETHING MORE THAN THAT.

HA HA HEE HOH!
YOU ARE DEFEATED!
NOTHING CAN SAVE YOU NOW!
KLANG!
AHRG!
MY CHEST ARMOR!
SMASHED!
WHO DARES...?
STEP AWAY FROM THE SUPER FAMILY!
WHAT?!
YOU FOOLISH MAN OF STEEL! YOUR HAMMER CAN NOT HARM ME!

AND YOUR KRYPTONITE POWERS WON'T WORK ON ME, VILLAIN!
OH, YEAH?
WE'LL SEE ABOUT THAT!
FLY FLY
CHARGE RUN
EVIL RUN RUN TROT
CRASH!
KLANG!

THANK YOU, NATASHA!
THE EFFECTS OF THE KRYPTONITE SEEM TO BE WEARING OFF!
WITH ALL THAT KRYPTONITE, I CAN'T RISK GETTING NEAR HIM!
HOWEVER...
...I HAVE SOMETHING I CAN USE BACK AT THE FORTRESS!
THANKS, NATASHA!
WE'LL BE RIGHT BACK!
SO, WHAT'S HE UP TO?
OH, I'M SURE HE HAS A PLAN.
YOU ARE FINISHED, STEEL MAN!
YOUR SUPER FRIENDS HAVE ABANDONED YOU!
PREPARE FOR YOUR DOOM!
WHAT?
GRAB!

SUPERMAN!
WHAT IS THIS?!
IT'S MY SUPER-MOBILE!
ARF ARF!
IT'S BUILT FROM LEAD TO HELP SHIELD ME FROM YOUR DEADLY RAYS, METALLO!
HEY!
AND THIS LEAD BOX WILL SHIELD YOU FROM EVERYTHING ELSE!
A LITTLE HEAT VISION TO SEAL THE DEAL!
HEY!
THANK YOU, JOHN!
NICE HAMMER USAGE.
THANKS.
NICE LEAD SUITS.
THANK YOU, SIR.
CURSE YOU, SUPERMAN!
LET ME OUT OF HERE!

THIS IS FOR YOU, JOHN.
WELCOME TO THE FAMILY!
THANK YOU!
CALL ME STEEL!
NICE!
HHMM... SOMETHING IS STILL MISSING.
HERE, DR. IRONS, ONE MORE THING TO MAKE YOU COMPLETE!
NICE TOUCH!
SUPER FAMILY!
SOLOMON GRUNDY IS RAMPAGING THROUGH THE CITY!
THIS LOOKS LIKE A JOB FOR...
US!
HELLO?
ANYBODY?
WHEN YOU GONNA LET ME OUTTA HERE?
-BOXED IN!

SUPERMAN FAMILY ADVENTURES
MEANWHILE, AT THE KENT FARM IN SMALLVILLE...
FINALLY! A NICE, CLEAN FARM.
KENT
WHAM!
OH, HI MOM!
CLARK?! I JUST CLEANED UP ALL THE HAY!
YOU JUST MADE A MESS!
SORRY, MA. FIGHTING BAD GUYS!
GOTTA GO!
WELL, THAT'S NOT FAIR.
MANY MINUTES LATER...
AH. CLEAN ONCE AGAIN.
WHAM!
CLARK!
HI, AUNT MARTHA!
IT'S ME, CONNER!
WELL, CONNER, YOU TELL THOSE BAD GUYS TO STOP THROWING YOU AND YOUR COUSINS INTO THE BARN!

I'LL TRY.
MMM.
MANY MORE MINUTES LATER...
WHEW! FINALLY!
WHAM!
HI, AUNT MARTHA!
WHO'S DOING THIS TO YOU?!
SOLOMON GRUNDY.
BYE, AUNTIE!
CURSE YOU, GRUNDY!
BUS STOP
METROPOLIS BUS LINES

—DEFINITELY NOT A MONDAY.

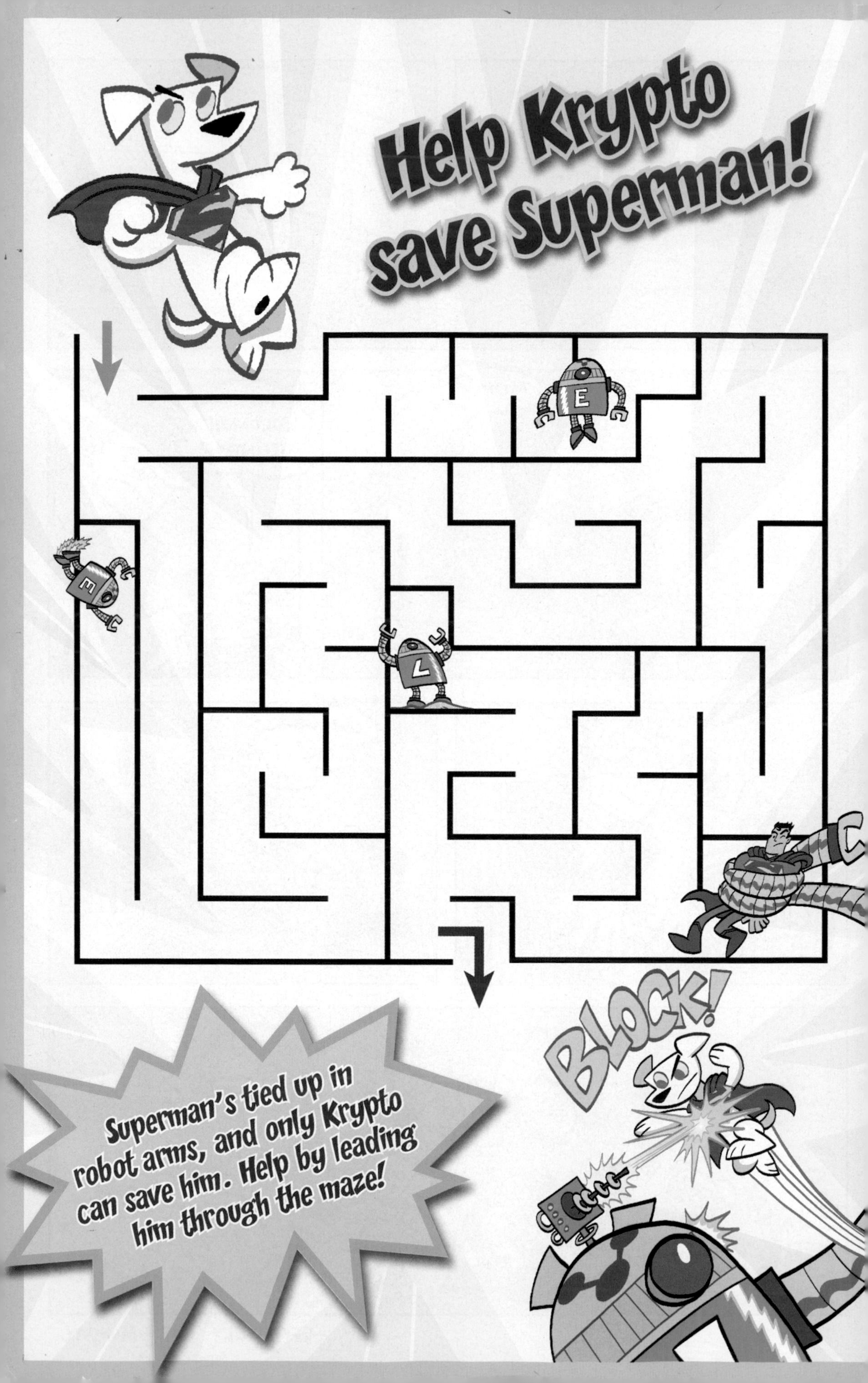
Help Krypto save Superman!
E
E
L
BLOCK!
Superman's tied up in robot arms, and only Krypto can save him. Help by leading him through the maze!